Email:  hello@CoopChaos.com

# www.CoopChaos.com

A CIP catalogue record of this book is available in the British Library

ISBN: 9798608277023

Typeface: Grundschrift by Christian Urff

# meet the hens

Bluebell

Buttercup

Dear children,

We hope that you enjoy reading our book Morning Mystery from the Coop Chaos book series. We wrote and illustrated these books for our grandchildren, whom we love very much. We hope that everyone who reads the Coop Chaos books enjoy them as much as we have enjoyed making them.

We dedicate this book to our wonderful grandchildren and to you our readers.

Thank you

Alyson Oliver (author) and
Derek Maguire (illustrator)

# MORNING MYSTERY

# Alyson Oliver & Derek Maguire

Daisy shivered; the coop was very cold this morning.

"Move over everyone," she clucked, "so there is room for me amongst the nice warm straw."

Poppy spread her wings and flapped them about noisily, taking up even more space on the perch, where five of the six hens were huddled together on this cold December morning.

Buttercup and Bluebell began to fidget, first standing on one leg and then on both legs. Lily and Rose the smallest of the hens started to cluck and crow loudly.

'Why was there so much fuss?' thought Daisy, 'why was it not possible for them all to live happily together instead of the constant arguing?' This always resulted in Daisy having to sleep alone in the cold part of the Coop. A sudden noise coming from the roof of the coop disturbed the six hens. It was not a sound they knew. It was a gentle pitter-patter on the roof.

Poppy listened carefully; the others would expect her to know what this sound might be. After all, she was supposed to be the cleverest. As she listened, she tried very hard to decide what this strange sound might be. It didn't sound like rain and it most certainly didn't sound like hailstones. She knew it wasn't the wind for that was quite a different sound altogether.

Buttercup was looking nervous; she was the biggest worrier amongst the group and her timid nature often made her a victim of Daisy's cruel jokes. She looked to Poppy for the answer of the mystery sound. What could it be?

Daisy was still shivering in her cold corner and feeling most annoyed that she had been sent there because of what she thought to be a simple mistake. She could not hold back her anger any longer.

"Well Poppy," she clucked, "has the fox got your tongue. It isn't like you not to know the answer to a mystery?"

Daisy was enjoying this. She liked being silly and naughty. At times, she could even be very funny, much to the amusement of the other hens. All except Poppy who was never amused with Daisy.

Poppy kept listening to the soft pitter-patter on the roof and began to observe the sunlight creeping in through the window. 'What's that?' she thought as she saw large white fluffy flakes falling from the sky. 'It didn't look scary; in fact, it looked quite lovely,' she thought.

Poppy called the others to look towards the window. For a long time, they all peacefully stared at the large white fluffy flakes falling from the sky. Even Daisy was astonished to the point of being unusually quiet.

Once again, they looked to Poppy for the answer. She decided that the mysterious sound and the sight through the window were somehow connected, but she didn't know how. Everyone was getting hungry. Bluebell began to fret; she stretched her neck and began moving her head from side to side. Rose who always seemed to be hungry, was getting restless too.

Daisy was feeling cold, so she ruffled and plumped her feathers to try to get warm. 'Where was Mr Green?' she thought, he usually came to feed them and let them out of the coop just after first light, and when he didn't come, his sister would look after their needs instead. They knew Mr Green and his sister took their eggs but none of them minded for they loved the two of them for always giving them food, water, treats and, a nice clean coop to sleep in. Yes, they were very kind to them and all but Daisy tried their best to be well behaved to show their respect in return.

Buttercup who was always kind and gentle, began to feel sorry for Daisy. The temperature in the coop was dropping very low and she herself had never felt so cold.

The five hens with their feathers plumped up and all of them huddled closely together offered some warmth to one another, but Daisy had no one to snuggle up to.

She asked the others to move over and make room for Daisy and to be kind to her. Luckily for Daisy they agreed and so she was allowed to join the other hens on the perch. They stayed together like this for a long time, well past the time Mr Green usually came, and still the white fluffy flakes fell pitter-patter on the roof.

At last they heard a strange crunching sound from outside the coop and they recognised the voice of Mr Green as he shouted to Mr Dale on the next garden.

"Hi, it looks like it's been snowing all night by the depth of this snow. I had all on getting out of my house this morning," he shouted to Mr Dale, who was on the next allotment.

Mr Dale answered by saying that the temperature had now dropped to minus nine and if the snow didn't let up soon, he doubted if he would manage to return in the evening to feed his pigs.

'What was this snow they were talking about?' thought Poppy. And within moments they were about to find out. They all knew the morning routine. Mr Green unlocked the big wooden gate leading into the long and safe compound where they had the freedom to run around and check out every corner that they were able to reach.

Once inside the compound, he would unlock the small hatch door of the coop, allowing them all to have the freedom to play together outside or to remain inside if they wished.

They all recognised the sound of the hatch door being unlocked, which filled them with excitement every morning. But this morning their excitement was filled with wonder for all of them, except Buttercup, who was a little afraid of what Mr Green and Mr Dale meant by the word snow.

The size of the hatch door was only big enough for one of them at a time to go through, and knowing this, they always tried to be patient with each other so as not to get hurt trying to squeeze through together.

Daisy had been thinking about this while alone in her corner and she intended to be the first one out of the hatch and into the compound so she could be the first of the hens to see what Mr Green and Mr Dale meant by the word snow.

Quick as a flash she jumped off the perch flapping her wings and made her way to the hatch entrance, pushing in front of poor bluebell who was small and timid.

Poppy let out a loud cheeping squawk so as to warn Daisy that she was not impressed once again with her bad behaviour. Rose flapped her wings in annoyance causing feathers and straw to fly into the air.

Daisy ran down the ladder. The others did not get the chance to follow for within seconds they heard a loud shriek from Daisy and the sound of wings flapping frantically. The other hens held back. They sensed danger. Was Mr Fox out there waiting for them? Surely not they decided. After all Mr Green was around and Mr Fox, sly and cunning only came at night.

Lily who was known for her bravery, popped her head through the hatch to investigate the situation. What she saw, both surprised her and made her cluck with glee. The others who were in an orderly line behind her became excited and desperate to know what had happened to Daisy?

Mr Green had heard the excited sounds inside the coop and had come to investigate. The others heard him laughing and scolding Daisy for being a naughty Hen.

"It's always you isn't it?" he said.

"If only you had been patient for a little while longer, I would have cleared away the snow from inside the compound. Now look what has happened to you! Trapped in the snow drift and unable to move. You, silly girl!"

They all looked up to Lily for an explanation and although Daisy was most annoying at times, they wished her no harm. Lily was enjoying this moment that her bravery had earned her and so she began to tell them of what she had seen.

"The whole garden and indeed the whole of the allotment had disappeared," she said. A loud gasp came from the other hens. How could this be they clucked.

"The gardens look beautiful. Everywhere is covered in a white sparkling blanket as though the stars have fallen from the sky," Lily told them and she began to enjoy being in the limelight.

"What about Daisy?" the others anxiously clucked.

She gleefully told them, "Daisy is stuck in a huge fold of the white blanket and Mr Green is trying to dig her out."

Poppy had finally worked out that the white blanket must be the snow that Mr Green and Mr Dale were speaking of. The mystery was solved. The white soft flakes must have knitted the white blanket to keep the garden warm she told the others.

"We knew you would know the answer to the mystery," they all clucked.

Later in the day when Mr Green had cleared away the blanket from the compound and returned a very cold and wet Daisy to the coop. The other hens led by Lily of course, slowly left the coop and saw for themselves the very pretty blanket of snow that mother nature had knitted for the allotment to keep it warm.

# THE END

# COMING SOON

Would you like to be the first to know when the next Coop Chaos book is published?

Ask a grown-up to sign-up to our e-newsletter via our website www.CoopChaos.com

Free kids activities at:

www.CoopChaos.com

# MEET THE CREATORS

## THE AUTHOR

As a child Alyson Oliver loved visiting her local library and spent hours reading books. When she grew-up, her love of books kept growing. After the birth of her first grandchild, she felt inspired to write stories for him and all her future grandchildren. Whilst observing her hens in her allotment, she noticed their personalities and devised the Coop Chaos book series with her friend Derek, the illustrator.

## THE ILLUSTRATOR

For many years Derek Maguire, has been painting for his family and friends in his attic studio. His favorite media is watercolours and has recently been teaching his grandchildren too. Derek has worked hard to showcase the Coop Chaos hen's personalities through his paintings. He looks forward to painting the next installment of Coop Chaos.

Printed in Great Britain
by Amazon